ISLAND STORMS

By Chantay Turner
Illustrated by Anton Syadrov

I0158492

Library For All Ltd.

There was a storm growing on Thursday Island.

No one could leave their houses.

When the rain started, it was heavy and hard.

The ocean churned.

Some people's dinghies
and boats were swept away.

Could there be a flood?

Already, there was wind, lightning and thunder.

The only safe place was inside and upstairs, but the storm had turned the power off.

The floodwater wasn't very high, so no one needed to escape to the roof.

11

But no one could check the news.

They had no idea how long the storm would last, or how much damage it would cause.

13

Suddenly, the lightning stopped.

So some people thought the storm was leaving.

15

But it got worse!

And the ocean swelled
uncontrollably.

It lasted all night, until the sun came out the next day.

The people on the island were relieved.

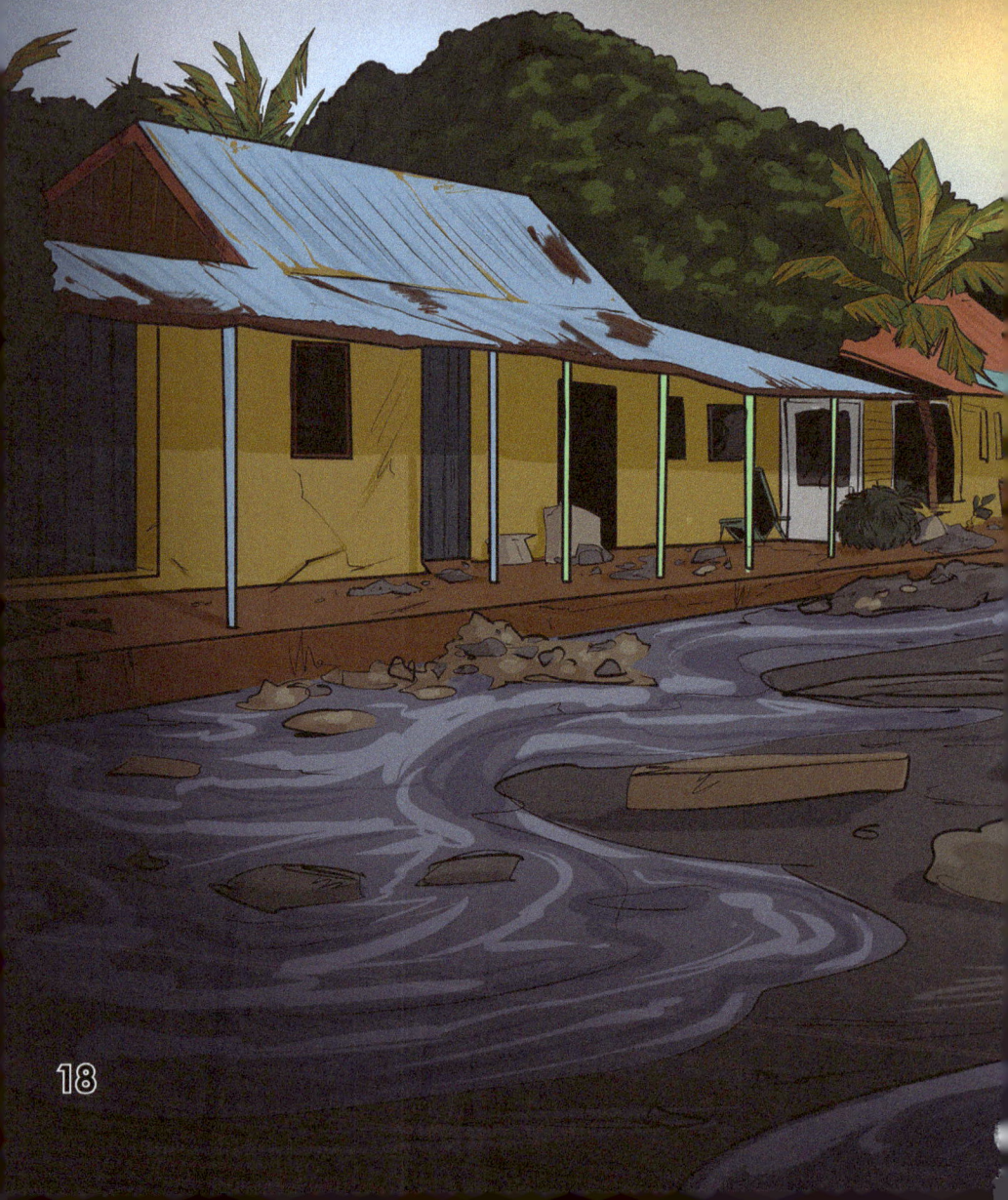

19

Everyone was happy the storm was over.

There was a lot of cleaning up to do, and everyone in the community helped out!

Stay safe in a storm

1

Stay inside until the storm has stopped.

2

Stay out of floodwater, as there could be dangers beneath the surface.

3

Stay away from windows, in case of hail or flying debris.

4

Stay away from trees, as they could fall over or they could be hit by lightning.

5

Stay away from fallen power lines or electrical equipment, as they could be dangerous.

6

Stay up to date. Use a radio to hear any important information or announcements.

7

Stay in contact with your neighbours, to make sure they are safe too.

You can use these questions to talk about this book with your family, friends and teachers.

What did you learn from this book?

Describe this book in one word. Funny? Scary? Colourful? Interesting?

How did this book make you feel when you finished reading it?

What was your favourite part of this book?

Download the Library For All Reader app from libraryforall.org

About the author

Chantay Turner is from Thursday Island and loves watching TV and playing games with family. Chantay's favourite book as a child was *The Hungry Caterpillar*.

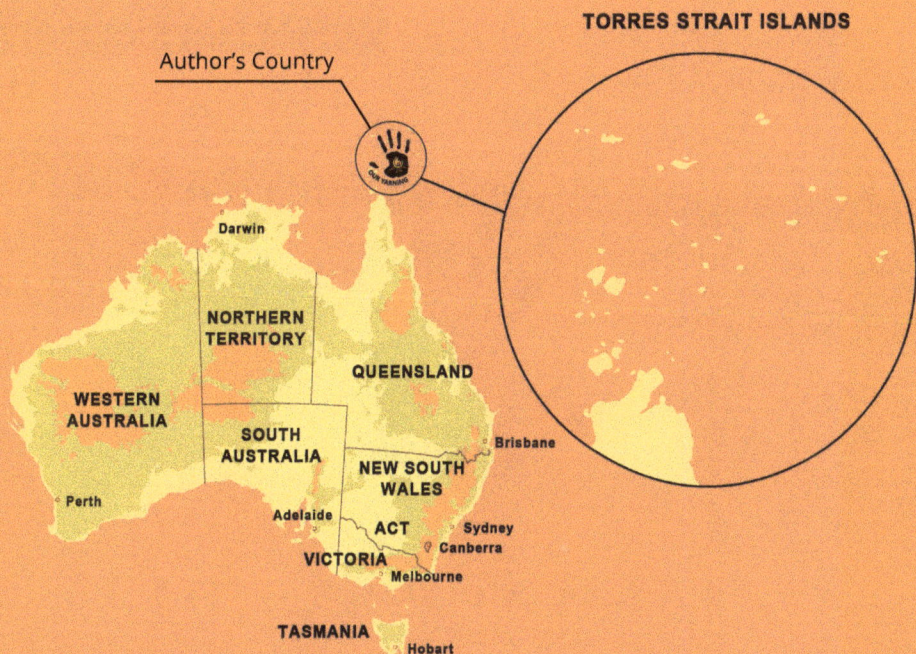

Author's Country

TORRES STRAIT ISLANDS

Darwin

NORTHERN TERRITORY

QUEENSLAND

WESTERN AUSTRALIA

SOUTH AUSTRALIA

Brisbane

NEW SOUTH WALES

Perth

Adelaide

ACT

Sydney

Canberra

VICTORIA

Melbourne

TASMANIA

Hobart

Our Yarning

The Our Yarning collection aligns with the Australian Curriculum through the Cross-Curriculum Priorities — Aboriginal and Torres Strait Islander Histories and Cultures. The collection provides an authentic opportunity for learning and embedding Aboriginal and Torres Strait Islander perspectives because it is written by Aboriginal and Torres Strait Islander people.

We know that children learn better, and enjoy reading more, when they see themselves in the stories, characters and illustrations of the books they read.

To download the app, visit the Google Play Store or Apple Store and search 'Our Yarning'.

You're reading Level 3

Learner – Beginner readers

Start your reading journey with short words, big ideas and plenty of pictures.

Level 1 – Rising readers

Raise your reading level with more words, simple sentences and exciting images.

Level 2 – Eager readers

Enjoy your reading time with familiar words, but complex sentences.

Level 3 – Progressing readers

Develop your reading skills with creative stories and some challenging vocabulary.

Level 4 – Fluent readers

Step up your reading skills with playful narratives, new words and fun facts.

Middle Primary – Curious readers

Discover your world through science and stories.

Upper Primary – Adventurous readers

Explore your world through science and stories.

Library For All is an Australian not for profit organisation with a mission to make knowledge accessible to all via an innovative digital library solution. Visit us at libraryforall.org

Island Storms

First published 2024

Published by Library For All Ltd
Email: info@libraryforall.org
URL: libraryforall.org

This book was created in collaboration with Yalari to improve and support the educational outcomes of First Nations children in Australia. We thank Yalari for their ongoing support of the Our Yarning program.

Educating Indigenous Children

Our Yarning logo design by Jason Lee, Bidjipidji Art

Original illustrations by Anton Syadrov

Island Storms
Turner, Chantay
ISBN: 978-1-923207-30-1
SKU04411

www.ingramcontent.com/pod-product-compliance
Lightning Source LLC
Chambersburg PA
CBHW042342040426
42448CB00019B/3373